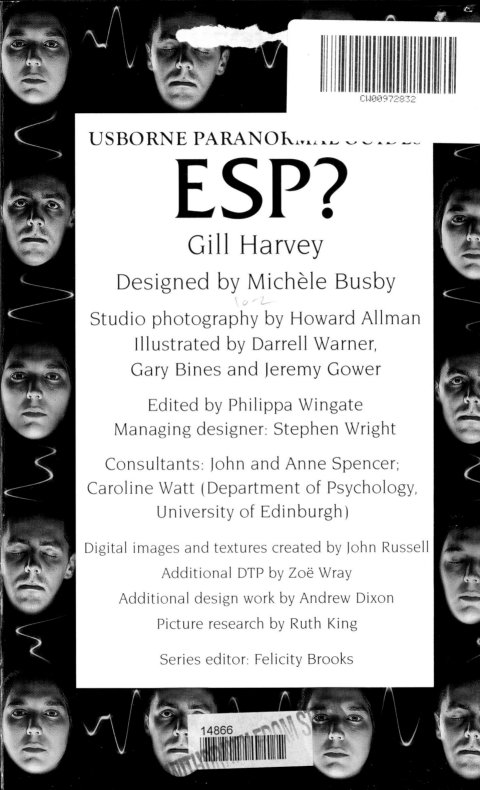

ESP?

Gill Harvey

Designed by Michèle Busby

Studio photography by Howard Allman
Illustrated by Darrell Warner,
Gary Bines and Jeremy Gower

Edited by Philippa Wingate
Managing designer: Stephen Wright

Consultants: John and Anne Spencer;
Caroline Watt (Department of Psychology,
University of Edinburgh)

Digital images and textures created by John Russell
Additional DTP by Zoë Wray
Additional design work by Andrew Dixon
Picture research by Ruth King

Series editor: Felicity Brooks

CONTENTS

WHAT IS ESP?

Have you ever "known" that a friend is about to telephone you, or had a dream which later comes true? If you have, you may have experienced ESP, or extrasensory perception. "Extra" is another way of saying outside or beyond, so ESP means experiences we couldn't have had via our senses (sight, hearing, smell, taste and touch). Most scientists believe that we learn all we know through our senses. However, if ESP exists, it's possible that we learn things in other, more mysterious ways.

Case studies

There are seven case studies in this book which describe fascinating accounts of ESP. Like most accounts of strange happenings, they are based on the claims of the people involved, and on how the stories have been passed on since. So how can you be sure they're true?

The answer is that no one can be sure. Factors such as coincidence, and the way we remember or imagine things, can cast doubts on people's accounts. In some cases, the stories may even have been made up.

You will find assessments after each case study. They outline some of these factors, so that you can decide for yourself whether or not you believe the stories.

Understanding ESP terms

There are specific names for different kinds of ESP, which you will come across throughout the book.

Telepathy means communication between minds. A simple example is knowing that a friend is thinking of phoning you.

Clairvoyance is when someone "sees" information about an object or event, without receiving this information from another mind. An example might be visualizing where to find a lost set of keys.

A premonition is a warning about something bad that is going to happen in the future – for example, a dream about a plane or a car that is going to crash.

People who claim to experience any kind of ESP on a regular basis are often described as psychic.

ESP and science

Some people are trying to discover whether ESP exists by using scientific experiments. This book describes some of these tests, and assesses how successful they have been so far.

You can also find out how to test your own ESP on pages 46-47.

Case study one: ARCTIC EXPEDITION

Date: 1937
Place: New York, USA; the Arctic

THE EVENTS

If a person was lost in the Arctic without a radio, would he be able to get help by sending thoughts across the icy wastes?

One evening in 1937, a famous explorer, Sir Hubert Wilkins, was in a club in New York. He was approached by a writer named Harold Sherman, who asked him exactly this question.

A challenging idea

Wilkins was about to start an expedition to look for a crashed plane in the Arctic. The two men chatted about the communication problems he might have, and joked about how telepathy would be the perfect solution. Then the idea dawned on them: why not use this opportunity to see if they *could* communicate by telepathy?

Devising a test

They came up with the following experiment: three nights a week, between 11:30pm and midnight, New York time, Wilkins would send mental impressions of his day to Sherman. At the same time, Sherman would write down what thoughts came into his mind. He would then send a copy to

a researcher named Dr. Gardner Murphy, who would give it to a lawyer for safe keeping. Wilkins would also keep a record of his experiences. When he got back to New York, the two accounts would be compared.

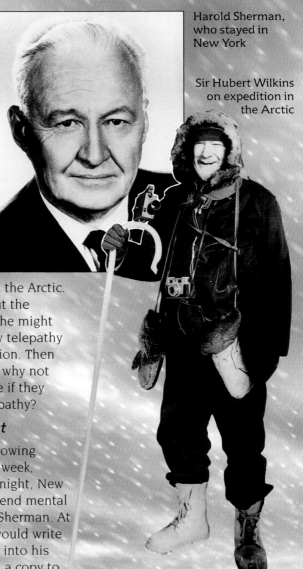

Harold Sherman, who stayed in New York

Sir Hubert Wilkins on expedition in the Arctic

Vivid impressions

In total, there were 68 telepathy sessions, during which Sherman received many strikingly vivid images of the expedition. There was one of an Eskimo funeral, one of Wilkins' plane, and another of a road next to a river bank.

Another impression, which he felt unable to explain, was that of a fire. Was it a fire on the ice? As the image became clearer, he saw it was a white house near Wilkins' camp. It was burning fiercely, and people were gathered around it, staring. The flames shot up in the freezing cold air while a sharp wind blew.

Sherman saw a vision of a white house on fire.

An unlikely evening

Another impression was of a dramatic series of events. Sherman felt that Wilkins' plane had been caught in a snowstorm on his way north, and that he was forced to land at a place named Regina. This in itself was quite likely. Next, he had an image of Wilkins at a ball – in full evening dress. This seemed unbelievable for a man on an expedition.

However, Sherman could even see a room full of men and women in evening dress, so he wrote his impressions down.

On Wilkins' return, Sherman's impressions were put to the test.

One night Sherman had an impression of Wilkins drinking unusual wine.

Another image was of people playing table tennis.

Case study one: ARCTIC EXPEDITION

Amazing results

The results of the experiment were stunning. Time and time again, Sherman's impressions had been right. The most amazing account of all was the story about the ball. The account below, based on Wilkins' log book, demonstrates how accurate Sherman's version was:

This morning took off on flight. Hoping to reach Saskatchewan. Was caught in heavy blizzard. Propose to turn back and make a landing in Regina.

Was met at the airport by the Governor of the province who invited me to attend an officers' ball being held there that evening.

My attendance at this ball was made possible by the loan to me of an evening dress suit.

Sherman went on to write books about ESP.

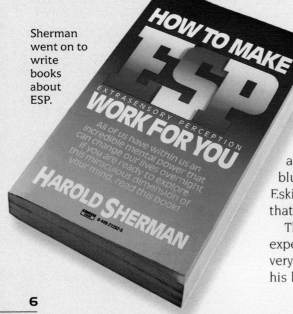

Matching details

Many of Sherman's other impressions were also correct. The fire he had seen turned out to be an Eskimo's shack burning. Members of the expedition had played table tennis in a school gym one evening, and on another evening Wilkins had tried blueberry wine. There had been an Eskimo child's funeral on the day that Sherman specified.

The astounding results of this experiment affected Harold Sherman very deeply. As a result, he devoted his life to psychic research.

This experiment seems to be a classic demonstration of telepathy at work. There seems little doubt that the two accounts were similar. But could there be any other explanations?

Inaccuracies

The impressions Sherman received were not completely accurate. For example, he thought that the Eskimo funeral was for an adult, not a child, and he pictured the shack fire 800km (500 miles) from where it really happened. He also failed to pick up any impressions of Wilkins' last flight to look for the crashed plane.

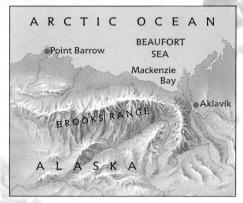

A R C T I C   O C E A N

BEAUFORT
SEA

Point Barrow

Mackenzie
Bay

Aklavik

BROOKS RANGE

A L A S K A

The shack fire actually happened at Point Barrow, not Aklavik, as Sherman thought.

Imagination and guesswork

Many images which Sherman described were of local people and landscapes. Sherman was a writer, and probably very imaginative.

This, together with the fact that he must have had a good idea of what the Arctic was like, could explain many of his impressions. However, it is still difficult to explain the more unusual incidents, or the times when the dates for each event apparently matched up in the two accounts.

Did the men cheat?

The fact that the experiment was monitored by other people would have made cheating difficult. Sherman could, perhaps, have received information from another member of the expedition. This is unlikely, as little information was available about the expedition until it was over.

Cheating is also unlikely because both men were well-known and respected, and neither would have wanted to spoil his reputation.

All in the interpretation?

Both men believed in ESP and wanted their experiment to succeed, so they may have read too much into the similarities between the accounts.

It is unclear what happened to the original diary and log book. What *is* known is that Sherman wrote pages and pages of impressions, probably far more than Wilkins wrote in his log book. The men may have picked out the few events in Sherman's account which matched the log book, and then interpreted the other slight similarities as successes as well.

COINCIDENCE

Imagine being in a foreign country on holiday and unexpectedly bumping into an old friend. What would you think? Would you think that it had happened by chance, or that it had happened for a reason?

Different perspectives

A coincidence is when two or more unrelated things connect unexpectedly. It's the word that people use when they believe these events have happened by chance.

Some people think that very few events are coincidences. They believe that there has to be a reason for the strange connections which happen in life. Some think that ESP can explain many seemingly coincidental events.

Other people think that unlikely events are bound to happen every now and again. Research has shown that we find it hard to believe when coincidences happen to us personally; but we are less surprised when they happen to someone else.

An unlikely story

The event described here is a good example of something which seems very unlikely. It happened on a London Underground train in 1971.

A passenger suddenly pressed the emergency button to stop the train. Strangely, the train was already stopping.

What the passenger didn't know was that someone suffering from a nervous breakdown had thrown himself in front of the train. The train driver had seen him jump, and managed to stop the train just in time. The man was only slightly injured.

The passenger couldn't explain why he had pressed the emergency button.

Was it a coincidence?

Once inside the train, the passenger wouldn't have been able to see anything happening in front of it – but it's possible that he knew by ESP that the train should stop.

The train driver would have braked suddenly when he saw the man jump. Could the sudden braking have caused the passenger to panic and press the button?

Case study two: PSYCHIC DETECTIVES

If ESP really exists, we may be able to use it to trace people, exchange news, or even solve crimes.

Date: 1974
Place: London, UK

THE STOLEN PAINTING

In 1974, a famous painting called *The Guitar Player* by Vermeer was stolen

Nella Jones

from Kenwood House in London.

When psychic detective Nella Jones heard the news, a map-like picture began to form in her mind.

The *Guitar Player* by Vermeer was taken out of its frame by the thieves.

"X" marks the spot

Nella sketched the picture and marked two crosses on it. She phoned the police and told them exactly where to find the picture frame. They followed her directions, and found it. Then she said that a lake near Kenwood held some more evidence. Indeed, the police found the picture's alarm mechanism at the edge of the water, where the thieves had thrown it.

Next, Nella told them that the picture would be found in a cemetery, unharmed. To their amazement, this also turned out to be true.

Was she guilty?

The police were so astonished at the accuracy of Nella's information that they wondered if she had been involved in the theft herself. When they found the real thieves, however, they cleared her name.

Kenwood House, the site of the crime

Case study two: PSYCHIC DETECTIVES

> **Date: The late 1970s**
> **Place: Yorkshire, UK**

THE YORKSHIRE RIPPER

Nella's reputation as a psychic grew over the next few years. When, in the 1970s, a man known as the Yorkshire Ripper was carrying out gruesome murders of women in Northern England, Nella came forward again.

Nella made many claims about the Ripper. For over a year, she gave impressions of who he was and what he did. She said he was a truck driver, and that his name was Peter.

Letters, names and numbers all came into Nella's mind.

She saw the letter C painted on the side of his truck, and said that he lived in Bradford. Nella even claimed to know what number house he lived in – number six. She predicted that he would murder someone with the initials J.H., and said he would strike again on November 17th or 27th, 1980.

The Ripper's arrest

On November 17th, 1980, a woman named Jaqueline Hill was killed by the Ripper. She was his last victim. He was finally arrested in January 1981. His name was Peter Sutcliffe, and he was indeed a truck driver, for a company called T. & W.H. Clark. He lived in Bradford, and his address was 6 Garden Lane.

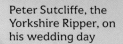

Peter Sutcliffe, the Yorkshire Ripper, on his wedding day

Date: 1958
Place: Florida, USA

FLORIDA MURDERS

In 1958, a psychic named Peter Hurkos was contacted by the police in Miami, Florida. A taxi cab driver had been shot in his cab, and the police were at a loss for clues.

The police took Hurkos to the cab, and he sat inside. He absorbed the atmosphere, touching the steering wheel and the dashboard.

Impressions began to form in his mind: the killer was tall and slim, and came from Detroit; he had a tattoo; his friends called him Smitty. Then Hurkos dropped a bombshell; this wasn't the only murder. There had been another. This man had killed someone else in Key West, another part of Florida.

Hurkos claimed to receive information through his hands.

Matching bullets

The police checked with their colleagues in Key West. Hurkos was absolutely right; another man had been shot, and the bullets in his body were from the same gun as those found in the cab driver's body.

Peter Hurkos

The Miami police worked on the details that Hurkos had given them, and contacted their colleagues in Detroit. They managed to piece together enough information to lead them to a man named Charles Smith. He was arrested and went to trial, where he was found guilty of both murders.

Date: 1962-1964
Place: Boston, USA

THE BOSTON STRANGLER

When horrific stranglings started happening in Boston, the police called in Hurkos again. They showed him photos of the crimes, and stockings and scarves that had belonged to the victims.

Hurkos studied the photos and touched the scarves and stockings. Very quickly, he began to build a picture of the murderer.

Hurkos let his mind run free as he touched the scarves and stockings.

Using touch in this way is known as psychometry (see page 26).

Conflicting views

Hurkos claimed that the murderer was fairly short, had a pointed nose, a scar on his left arm, and that he used to work with diesel engines. Hurkos himself believed a shoe salesman to be the Strangler. However, after a long hunt, the police decided they didn't agree with him. A schizophrenic named Albert DeSalvo confessed to the crimes, and the police accepted his confession.

Albert DeSalvo being escorted by a police officer following his arrest

Mistaken identity?

DeSalvo fitted the description Hurkos had given to the police. He had a pointed nose, a scar on his arm and he used to work with diesel engines. Yet Hurkos still insisted that the shoe salesman was the real culprit. Who was right? DeSalvo's mental health was too poor for him to go on trial, so the police never proved he was the killer. After his arrest, however, the stranglings stopped.

Case study two: THE ASSESSMENT

Whenever there is a dramatic crime or series of crimes, police detectives are often approached by psychics offering help. This can cause more problems than it solves. Valuable police time is used to follow up suggestions, which are often worthless. However, Nella Jones and Peter Hurkos have both been praised by some police officers for their help.

Hit and miss

One of the problems faced by the police is that psychic information is often hit and miss. For example, Nella was apparently very precise when she located the stolen painting, but she was a lot less precise about the Ripper. She suggested the name Peter, but she also suggested Harry, Charles and Leonard. She was right about his house number, but she thought his street was called Chapel Street. She also claimed, wrongly, that the Ripper would strike again after the murder of Jaqueline Hill.

Too vague?

Although the Miami police found Hurkos helpful in the cab driver case, the Boston police were clearly not so sure about his views on the Boston Strangler. If anything, the disagreement showed that the sort of information he could give was too vague – it could be applied to too many people.

Psychic technique

Nella Jones admitted to some of the wrong guesses that she made about the Ripper. It's unusual, however, for psychics to do this. Research has shown that psychics often work by making many guesses; if they make enough, some are bound to be right. They then emphasize the right ones and downplay the wrong ones (people aren't interested in wrong guesses, anyway). They are also helped by the fact that major crimes are covered in a sensational way by the media, who are only too ready to listen to a psychic's claims.

Psychic detectives often benefit from media coverage, such as the newspaper stories shown here.

MYSTERY OF THE MISSING MUM

Psychic gives clue to body in lake

A TOP clairvoyant claims that Linda Sturley—a mother who vanished two years ago—has been murdered and her body dumped in a reservoir.

Now police chiefs may send in a team of divers to drag the 40ft-deep man-

By JEFF EDWARDS

an anonymous phone call told her, "She's in reservoir." and hung up "I want the police reserv...

SHE'S THE CLAIRVOYANT CRIME-BUSTER

Charlady Nella helps police mop up the vital clues

by PAUL SHAW

Clairvoyant Nella Jones returns

ESP – HISTORY AND SCIENCE

Ancient records show that people have believed in psychic experiences, such as premonitions, for thousands of years. However, terms such as ESP and telepathy have not existed very long. They were only invented as interest in psychic happenings grew.

F.W.H. Myers, one of the founders of the SPR, who invented the term "telepathy"

A 19th-century obsession

In the 19th century, many people in Europe and America claimed to have psychic experiences. The more people talked about them, the more they seemed to happen. At first, most of the claims were about contacting the spirit world, and the obsession became known as Spiritualism. As the craze grew, it came to include other phenomena such as reading minds or hypnotizing people.

A 19th-century seance. People claimed to contact spirits at meetings like this.

Serious investigation

By the 1880s, many Spiritualists had been shown to be frauds. However, some people started to think that there might sometimes be a scientific explanation for the experiences.

In 1882, a group of Spiritualists and scientists set up the Society for Psychical Research (SPR) in London, to investigate people's claims.

The SPR started to put psychic experiences into different categories. Two of the categories were clairvoyance and mind reading. One of the SPR's founders, F.W.H. Myers, gave mind reading a new name – telepathy.

The SPR also collected thousands of accounts of psychic experiences, many of which were published together in a book called *Phantasms of the Living*.

Finding a test

The SPR's work was significant because, for the first time, psychic experiences were treated rationally. While the society gathered many interesting stories, however, this was not enough to prove that they had really happened. Early in the 20th century, scientists started to think of ways to test people's psychic ability.

Dr. Joseph Rhine

In 1934, a scientist called Dr. Joseph Rhine gave a new name to phenomena such as clairvoyance and telepathy – he called them extrasensory perception, or ESP.

He also developed new ways of testing for them. He realized that ESP could only be proven to exist in strictly monitored experiments. Cheating should be completely ruled out, and the results should be clearly analyzed.

Dr. Rhine worked in the Parapsychology Laboratory of Duke University, North Carolina, USA

Zener cards

Dr. Rhine often used a pack of cards called Zener cards. In one experiment, he would choose cards at random and ask the "subject" (the person being tested for ESP) to guess which he had chosen. For the experiment to work, he had to show that the subjects guessed the correct cards (known as the "targets") more often than chance could account for.

These are the five different symbols in a pack of Zener cards.

Results and criticism

These experiments seemed to succeed in demonstrating ESP, and they attracted a lot of attention. However, when other scientists tried to repeat them, they didn't get the same results. Many began to question whether Dr. Rhine had monitored his experiments strictly enough.

Case study three: FREEZING TO DEATH

Date: 1994
Place: Oberammergau, Germany

THE EVENTS

The shadows grew longer as the sun began to sink. There was no sign of the right track. As Steve and Ian plodded on, and on, they began to realize that they were truly lost...

A skiing holiday

Ian Middleton and Steve Swindlehurst were staying in the village of Oberammergau in the Alps. They were experienced skiers, so they had decided to ski down a difficult track, known as a black run, on a nearby mountain. It was one which neither of them had tried before.

The black run disappears

When they had set off up the mountain, it was a beautiful day. They'd reached the top and started skiing, skimming over the snow. But the black run wasn't marked very clearly, and suddenly, it seemed to come to an end. Steve and Ian were puzzled. They stopped and looked around. They soon realized they were on another track, somewhere deep in the middle of the forest.

Ian and Steve were surrounded by trees in every direction.

The two skiers weren't worried at first. They thought it would be easy to find their way back to the black run. But as they went on, and on, they realized they must have missed it altogether.

Freezing temperatures

On winter nights in the Alps, it's common for the temperature to drop to -20°C (-4°F). It's difficult for a human to survive a night at this temperature. Ian and Steve knew this, and that they should try to get down the mountain before it grew too cold. But the forest was dense, and it was getting dark.

Oberammergau village

They decided that their best hope would be to stay in one place, so that it would be easier for a search party to find them.

The hours tick by

It grew colder and colder. Ian and Steve made a "snow hole", a shelter in the snow, to keep warm in; but it didn't work very well. Gradually, they gave up hope of being found that night; they'd been missing for nearly eight hours. But they were determined to stay positive – they didn't dare think about freezing to death.

Case study three: FREEZING TO DEATH

Desperate rescuers

A rescue team had indeed been looking for them. In fact, they'd been hunting for hours, and were about to give up. The mountainside was huge and forbidding in the dark, and the skiers could be anywhere. But news of the search had spread around the village, and to one man in particular. His name was Georg Horak.

An ancient art

Georg was a dowser, known locally as "the man with the special gift". The ancient art of dowsing is a method of finding something – traditionally, underground water – using sticks or rods called dowsing rods. The rods move in the dowser's hands, either when he stands on the right spot (field dowsing) or when the rods

are over the right spot on a map (map dowsing). As a map dowser, Georg had located many things in his 73 years. Perhaps he could locate the skiers, too. He brought out a map and his rods.

The rods swing

Georg spread out his map, and began to move his rods over the area of the mountain. Suddenly, they swung together over one point. Georg moved them away. They swung apart. He moved them back, and they swung together again. There was no mistaking it – he'd located the skiers. He rushed to phone the rescue team. Fortunately, Georg was known well enough in the village for the team to take him seriously. They set off up the mountain again for one last try.

The dowsing rods crossed at a point less than 300m (1000ft) from the lost skiers.

Lights and voices

Ian and Steve were getting dangerously cold. They jumped up and down to keep warm, but nothing seemed to stop the cold from seeping deeper and deeper into their bones. Would anyone ever come?

When one of them thought they heard voices, it seemed too good to be true. They looked around. They couldn't see anything. They must have imagined it. Then, a few minutes later, they heard voices again, and saw flashlights through the trees. It *was* true – the rescuers had found them at last. They were safe!

A big news story

Ian and Steve's rescuers took them down into the village as fast as they could, without stopping to explain how they had found them. But later, the skiers found out that their rescue had become famous. A newspaper reporter phoned them and told them

In the dense, dark forest, it seemed incredible that the men had been found.

about Georg the dowser, and how the rescue team had reached the point of giving up when Georg had contacted them. Ian and Steve were amazed, and very, very grateful. They agreed to appear on German television to thank Georg for saving their lives.

Needle in a haystack

The leader of the mountain rescue team, a man named Alwin Delago, explained how amazing the rescue really was. The mountains behind Oberammergau are massive, and the trees make it difficult to see anything, especially in the dark. The chances of finding the men without Georg's help, he explained, would have been similiar to finding a needle in a haystack.

Case study three: THE ASSESSMENT

There's little doubt that Georg Horak helped the rescue team to find the skiers, but there may be a logical explanation for how he did it.

In-depth knowledge

Georg had lived in Oberammergau for many years. His knowledge of the mountain was probably very good indeed. The rescue team would have been under pressure and would have had little time to study a map calmly. It's possible, therefore, that it was Georg's knowledge of the mountain, and the time that he was able to spend looking at the map, that led him to pick the right area. It's also possible that he didn't consciously realize this himself.

Exaggeration

Georg may have made a lucky guess – after all, he only indicated a spot 300m (1000ft) from the skiers. It seems that the press made it sound as though he pinpointed them exactly, whereas it would have been quite easy for the rescue team to miss the men even with his directions.

Last flicker of hope

Without doubt, Georg's belief in his dowsing ability encouraged the rescue team when they were about to give up. Even if he did make a lucky guess, the skiers can still be grateful to him, because the rescuers may not have persevered without his advice.

This is a field dowser, looking for water. It's possible that this skill is based on clairvoyance.

ESP and other psychic skills

It's possible that dowsing works through a combination of telepathy and clairvoyance, and that dowsing rods are simply tools for focusing the mind's ESP.

ESP may also be at the root of other psychic skills. If so, it could cast doubt over them. For example, a medium (someone who claims to contact the dead) might be able to detect telepathically that someone is grieving, and who they are grieving for. The medium could then claim, fraudulently, that the dead person has sent a "message" to comfort the person who is still alive.

ESP – THE RIGHT CONDITIONS?

ESP testing continues to produce inconsistent results, and no one has proved conclusively that ESP exists. This may be because it only occurs under certain conditions.

Spontaneous happenings

Most people claim to experience ESP unexpectedly, in situations which are impossible to repeat. These experiences often seem to be triggered by dramatic or traumatic events, such as the ones described in the case studies in this book. This may be because our powers of ESP only really work when we need them, or at times of extreme emotion.

If so, laboratory tests may never be able to provide the right conditions for demonstrating ESP.

Factors in testing

While scientists can't recreate real-life trauma, they have done a lot of research on other factors which may influence people's performance in ESP tests – factors such as how they feel, or what they believe.

"Sheep" and "goats" are terms used to describe what people believe.

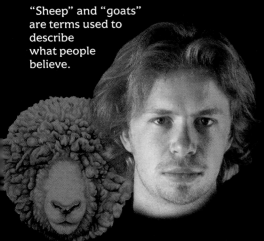

If you are a "goat", your belief that ESP tests don't work may lead to negative results.

Sheep and goats

In the 1950s, a scientist named Dr. Gertrude Schmeidler carried out a series of experiments which showed that people who believe in ESP tests do better in them than people who don't. She termed people who believe "sheep" and people who don't "goats".

Dreams and relaxation

Other scientists have found that people do better in ESP tests if they are feeling relaxed, or even when they're asleep. There's more about this on pages 27 and 45.

To test or not to test?

You may think that testing for ESP is pointless if scientists can't create exactly the right conditions. However, it's still not clear what these conditions may be. Until we know, testing is the only way to rule out other explanations for what people think is ESP.

Case study four: LOST IN THE ANDES

Date: October – December, 1972
Place: The Andes, South America

THE EVENTS

On October 13th, 1972, a plane went missing high in the Andes mountains in South America. There were 45 young men and women on board. A search was mounted, but there was no sign of the wreck. The passengers' families became frantic with worry, and began to do everything in their power to find the plane.

A difficult flight

The passengers on the plane, a Fairchild F-27, were mainly a rugby team from Uruguay, on their way to play a game in Santiago, Chile. As they had flown through the treacherous Planchon Pass in the Andes, bad weather had shaken the plane. Soon afterwards, however, the pilot thought they had cleared the mountains, and began to descend. Then, suddenly, the rocky mountainside loomed up, dangerously close. The wing of the plane clipped the rocks. It broke off, and the plane crashed down the mountain, breaking into pieces as it went.

This is the route taken by the plane. The weather was too bad to cross straight from Mendoza to Santiago, so the pilot had chosen to fly south to cross the mountains through the Planchon Pass, near Malargue.

Santiago
Mendoza
Curico
Malargue
Montevideo
URUGUAY
Planchon Pass
ARGENTINA
Intended flight path ------
CHILE

The plane hurtled down the mountain on its belly.

Survival

When the main body of the plane came to rest, many passengers were amazed to find that they were still alive and unharmed. Not everyone was so lucky. Some had died instantly, and some had serious injuries. However, of the 45 people on board, over 30 had survived.

The survivors were sure that help would come quickly. They tended to the injured as best they could, gathered together what food they could find among the wreckage and settled down to wait.

A desperate hunt

News that the plane had disappeared reached the passengers' relatives, and the Chilean Air Force Aerial Rescue Service started a search. They hunted for eight days, but found nothing – and gave up. The relatives couldn't believe the search had ended. What if their loved ones were still alive?

The rescue team's symbol

The old dowser

Some of the relatives decided to carry on searching themselves, and went to Chile to hunt for clues.

One woman went to an old dowser in Montevideo, Uruguay, instead. She took a map of the Andes with her. The old man's rods crossed over one area, and the woman noted where it was.

When her daughter, Madelon, gave this information to the other relatives, she was told that the area picked out by the dowser had already been searched by the rescue team. Disappointed, Madelon decided to try someone else.

The fuselage of the Fairchild plane in the snow, with a body lying outside it

Case study four: LOST IN THE ANDES

A famous psychic

Madelon found out about a famous psychic called Gerard Croiset. Unfortunately, he was ill, but his son, also called Gerard Croiset, offered to help as he claimed to have the same psychic abilities as his father. Madelon sent Croiset a map of the Andes and details of everything they knew about the plane's flight path.

Croiset's clues

A few days later, he phoned her. He said he felt that the co-pilot had been flying the plane alone, and that the plane had crashed 40 miles (65km) from the Planchon Pass. He was sure there were survivors.

One of the parents asked people who lived near the mountain to help hunt for the plane. As the days went by, Croiset sent more impressions. He described how the plane had broken into pieces. It had been heading for water – the sea, or a lake.

The relatives searched the area shown, prompted by Croiset's clues.

San Fernando · Tinguirica Volcano · CRASH SITE · Curico · PLANCHON PASS · Malargue

- Chilean rescue team's search
- The relatives' search
- ----- Actual flight path
- ----- Intended flight path

Croiset claimed the plane was near a village of white, Mexican-style houses.

He said the wreckage was hidden under an overhanging rock.

No progress

None of Croiset's clues led the relatives to the plane. After a while, Croiset himself gave up hope. He confessed that he now believed that everyone aboard the plane had died.

Starvation

Up on the mountain, the number of survivors was dwindling. Some had died of their injuries. Others had died when an avalanche swept over them. To make things worse, there was hardly any food left. They had only a few chocolates and some wine. Then they thought of something else – the bodies of the people who had died, preserved in the snow. They could use them for food. At first, this seemed a terrible idea, but as days went by, their hunger grew too great. They began to slice off pieces of flesh, and eat them.

Plan of escape

Weeks went by, but there was still no sign of a rescue team. The survivors tried climbing down the mountain, but found they had become too physically weak. The strongest among them were chosen to eat more of the human flesh to build up their strength. After several more weeks, they decided it was time to try again.

Success!

Against the odds, two of the survivors managed the treacherous journey down the mountain, and made contact with some villagers who lived in the valley below.

At the end of their incredible ordeal, the survivors had spent 10 long weeks on the mountain. There were 16 left alive.

The two who made it down the mountain being taken to safety.

Some of the survivors with their rescuers at the site of the crash.

Looking back

When the survivors were back home, their relatives assessed their search. Gerard Croiset's clues, they realized, had misled them. The plane hadn't been heading for water, and it wasn't hidden by an overhanging rock; and he had been wrong when he said that all the survivors had died. The plane had, however, broken into pieces as he had described, and there was a village which had white houses nearby.

The man they ignored

One person had got the location of the plane right – the old dowser from Montevideo. He had located the plane almost exactly. If his advice had been followed, there might have been more survivors, and the ordeal would have been over much sooner.

Case study four: THE ASSESSMENT

This case study shows some of the difficulties and dangers in using ESP as a means of gaining information. Even when some psychic impressions may turn out to be accurate in the end, they can be very difficult to interpret when they are first received.

The person who got it right

There is little doubt that the old water dowser in Montevideo hit upon the plane's location. As with most successes of this sort, it could be dismissed as a coincidence. However, what's certain is that some of the relatives of the crash victims wished they had taken more notice of what he had to say.

Croiset's guesses

Gerard Croiset's successes seem likely to have been lucky guesses, because so many of his suggestions turned out to be wide of the mark. Sceptics often point to the fact that if a psychic makes enough guesses, some of them are bound to be right.

Knowledge of events

It is perhaps not really surprising that Croiset thought he saw images such as the plane breaking up, or its remains hidden under a rock. Given that the plane had undoubtedly crashed, either possibility would be easy to imagine.

Psychometry

Gerard Croiset used a psychic technique known as psychometry. The psychic gets insight into a situation by touching things which are connected with it – in this case, for example, maps of the region. The original idea of psychometry was developed by a scientist named J. R. Buchanan, in the 1830s.

He suggested that objects record events or emotions, then transmit the information in some way.

Today, most psychometrists use objects simply to trigger their psychic powers. In other words, the power is believed to be in the psychic's mind, not in the object itself.

Psychometrists use their hands as a psychic tool.

ESP AND DREAMS

For thousands of years, theories have been suggested about what happens when people dream, because dreams seem to express so many secrets of the inner mind.

ESP and relaxed states of mind

ESP research has shown that being relaxed seems to increase ESP (see page 21). The one time when the mind is completely relaxed is during sleep. Some researchers had the idea that people's powers of ESP might, therefore, be at their greatest when they are dreaming.

The Maimonides laboratory

In the 1960s and 70s, researchers at the Maimonides Medical Center in New York carried out experiments to investigate ESP during dreams.

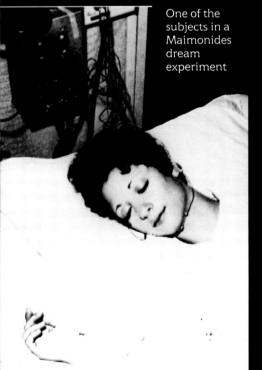

One of the subjects in a Maimonides dream experiment

In some of the experiments, one person slept while another person looked at a famous painting and tried to transmit it by ESP to the sleeper.

Using sophisticated brain scanning equipment (an electroencephalograph, or EEG), the testers monitored when the sleeper started dreaming.

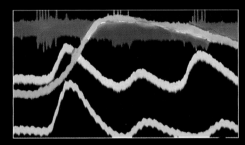

Graph lines produced by an EEG. By watching these lines, the testers could monitor the subjects' sleep patterns.

People only tend to remember a dream if they wake up in the middle of it, so the testers woke the sleeper after a few minutes of dream time.

The sleeper then related the dream into a tape recorder, and it was compared with the target painting.

Successful results

These were some of the most successful ESP experiments ever carried out. The sleepers often gave a good impression of the painting. But no one has managed to achieve the same level of success since, and very few ESP dream tests now take place.

One of the problems with dream testing, however, is the expense of using an EEG. As a result, scientists have developed the ganzfeld technique, which is less expensive (see page 45).

Case study five: THE *TITANIC*

Date: April 1912
Place: The Atlantic Ocean

THE EVENTS

The *Titanic*'s wireless operator would have had a room like this.

"*We have struck iceberg sinking fast come to our assistance.*" A desperate message came over the icy Atlantic waters. Then another: "SOS SOS W*e are sinking fast passengers being put into boats.*" Then a final, tragic plea – "*Women and children in boats cannot last much longer.*" The *Titanic*, the "unsinkable ship", was sinking on her first voyage. Just as so many people had foretold.

Jessie's vision

The *Titanic* had started out from the English port of Southampton for the journey across the Atlantic.

On the night of the disaster, back in England a little girl named Jessie lay dying. She was being cared for by Salvation Army Captain W. Sowden. Suddenly, she called for him.

"Hold my hand, Captain," she said. "I am so afraid. Can't you see that big ship sinking in the water?"

The Captain thought that Jessie must be becoming delirious.

"Don't worry, Jessie," he soothed her. "You're just having a bad dream."

"No," she insisted, in a frightened voice, "the ship is sinking. Look at all those people who are drowning." Then she added, "Someone called Wally is playing a fiddle."

The Captain was convinced that her fever was making Jessie imagine things. She was very ill, after all. Indeed, a few hours later, she died.

Is it possible that Jessie saw a scene like this?

Tragic music

Later on that night, the *Titanic* sank with the loss of over 1,500 lives. There were not enough lifeboats, and many people had to stay on the ship as it plunged deeper and deeper into the sea. While the passengers waited, terrified, for the icy water to engulf them, the ship's band tried to keep them from despair by playing cheerful tunes. The leader of the band was a man named Wally Hartley.

An old friend

When Captain Sowden heard about the *Titanic* sinking, he remembered Jessie's words. He also realized that he had once known the band leader, Wally. He had lost touch with him, and had no idea that he was serving on the liner.

A newspaper vendor after the tragedy

Case study five: THE *TITANIC*

Jessie's amazing vision made no difference to anyone on the ship. It didn't act as a warning to anyone. However, many who sailed that night *were* warned by people who had premonitions. Some passengers changed their bookings, but unfortunately, many ignored the warnings. Some of the warnings, in any case, came too late...

Blanche Marshall

A woman named Blanche Marshall and her husband decided to watch the famous *Titanic* sail off on her maiden voyage. After leaving Southampton, the ship was to pass the Isle of Wight, so a large crowd of people gathered there to watch. The Marshalls joined them.

The ship was an impressive sight, and everyone gazed in admiration and wonder. But suddenly, Blanche was seized with a terrifying feeling, and she cried out,

"That ship is going to sink before it reaches America!"

Embarrassment

People in the crowd turned to stare at Blanche. They thought she was crazy. After all, the Titanic was supposed to be unsinkable. Her husband tried to keep her quiet, but Blanche became more agitated. She started to shout:

"Do something!" she shrieked. "You fools! I can see hundreds of people struggling in the icy water. Are you all so blind that you are going to let them drown?"

The crowd was amazed at Blanche's outburst and her husband was embarrassed. He made her stay quiet, and the vast ship sailed past, on to its doom in the Atlantic.

The *Titanic* leaving the docks at Southampton with its escort of tugboats in April 1912.

Further warnings

Three years later, Blanche had another premonition, and this time her husband did not ignore her warning. In 1915, during the First World War, she and her husband had booked a trip for May of that year on another luxurious liner, the *Lusitania*.

A changed booking

Some time before they sailed, Blanche had the overwhelming feeling that the ship would be torpedoed and sunk by the German navy. Her husband had learned his lesson, and he immediately tried to change their booking. Unfortunately, the Marshalls were unable to change to another ship. The only option was to travel on the *Lusitania*, but earlier in the year.

Blanche had another terrifying vision of people in the water.

Strangely accurate

To her husband's surprise, Blanche agreed to the new arrangements. She explained that her premonition was very specific – the ship would not meet its end until May. She and her husband took the earlier trip and were unharmed.

Tragically, though, Blanche's prediction came true. When the *Lusitania* sailed off on its May voyage, it was indeed torpedoed by the Germans. It sank on May 7th, 1915, with the loss of over 1,000 lives.

The sinking of the *Lusitania* caused outrage in Britain and in America.

LEST WE FORGET

The Sinking of the Lusitania

Case study five: THE ASSESSMENT

Premonitions are very difficult to explain, because they involve the future. If they exist at all, something very strange must happen to time. Science still suggests that it's impossible for anyone to know about something which hasn't yet happened, or for a future event to jump back to the present.

Fear of travel?

People often feel scared before a voyage, because there is always an element of risk involved in travel. Blanche may have felt a similar fear on behalf of the people on the *Titanic*. Her vision of people struggling in the water may simply have been the result of a particularly lively imagination.

"EVERY ATTENTION GIVEN TO THE COMFORT AND SAFETY OF OUR PASSENGERS."

NEPTUNE.—You ought to go slower, my friend; there are many dangers about you! TRANS-ATLANTIC CAPTAIN OF THE PERIOD.—Can't help it; I 'm bound to make the fastest trip on record, and don't you forget it!

A late 19th-century cartoon warning about the dangers of travel

However, it's unlikely that Jessie would have known anything about the *Titanic*, so these explanations cannot account for her vision.

A dangerous boast

At the time, building the *Titanic* represented the highest pinnacle of human achievement. But to say that it was unsinkable seemed to be tempting fate. Some people may even have believed that a claim such as this was challenging God, and deserved to be punished.

As a result, people such as Blanche may have feared that such a boastful claim was bound to meet with disaster. They may have interpreted these anxieties as premonitions.

Psychic craze

The *Titanic* sank at a time when there was a craze for psychic experiences (see page 14). This makes it likely that stories of premonitions were exaggerated, or that people even made them up. For example, Jessie didn't name the *Titanic* in her vision. She just saw a big ship sinking. But Captain Sowden may have wanted to believe that she had seen the *Titanic*, and imagined that her feverish words had included the name Wally.

Similarly, the Marshalls may have exaggerated Blanche's original reaction on seeing the *Titanic* sail by, then built upon her reputation by telling the story about the *Lusitania*. There is no record of when the Marshalls told people about changing their booking, or indeed of why they changed their booking. They may have made up the story after the sinking of the *Lusitania*.

Case study six: THE RICH AND FAMOUS

ESP seems to be triggered by trauma or tragedies (you can find out more about this on page 21). Few deaths are as dramatic as the sudden death of a young, famous person.

> **Date: August 31st, 1997**
> **Place: Paris, France**

PRINCESS DIANA

Early in the morning on August 31st, 1997, news filtered through that Diana, Princess of Wales had been killed in a terrible car crash in Paris.

She was in the prime of life, and probably the most famous woman in the world. To many people, it seemed incredible that she had been killed. But there was someone who wasn't at all surprised.

Clairvoyant

Earlier in 1997, the chairman of the British UFO Research Association (BUFORA), Steve Gamble, was contacted by a woman who claimed to have had some premonitions which she wanted to be documented properly. Steve agreed to meet her.

A lengthy interview

They met on the weekend of August 24th, 1997, and Steve wrote down all the woman's predictions. Some of them were about events which had already happened, so it was impossible for Steve to check her story. However, one of her predictions was that Diana, Princess of Wales would die in a car crash within a year, and possibly sooner – within one or two months. To Steve's amazement, it was only a week before the prediction came true.

Diana, Princess of Wales. Most people were shocked by her death.

Case study six: THE RICH AND FAMOUS

Date: September 23rd, 1955
Place: Hollywood, USA

JAMES DEAN

In 1955, the actor James Dean was at the start of a great career. His first film, *East of Eden*, had been an instant hit, and his next, *Rebel Without a Cause*, made him a teenage idol. He lived an exciting life, and loved driving around in fast cars.

The Porsche Spider

In September 1955, James Dean bought a new sports car. It was sleek, stylish, and very powerful – a Porsche Spider. Excited by his purchase, James began to show it off to his friends. On September 23rd, he met fellow actor Alec Guinness in a restaurant.

Instant foreboding

Alec agreed to go outside to look at the car. The minute he saw the car he turned to James and said, "Please never get in it. It is now 10 o'clock Friday, September 23rd, 1955. If you get in that car you will be found dead in it by this time next week."

The horrific state of James Dean's Porsche Spider after the crash

James ignored Alec's request. He was far too excited about driving the Porsche to worry about what his friend had said. But the following Friday, almost exactly a week later, James did indeed meet his end. He had a horrendous crash in the Porsche and died instantly.

James next to the famous Porsche Spider

JOHN F. KENNEDY

Suddenly, as United States President John F. Kennedy was driven through the streets of Dallas, shots rang out. The President slumped forward. The marksman, whoever he was, had hit the spot. One bullet had hit the President's head, another his neck. He never regained consciousness.

A popular President

The assassination happened on Friday, November 22nd, 1963. The President had been in office for almost three years, having been voted in on November 9th, 1960.

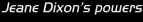

He was popular, and symbolized a new, youthful America. But someone had foreseen that his time in office would end in tragedy – as far back as 1952.

President Kennedy

Jeane Dixon's powers

Jeane Dixon was used to seeing visions. One morning in 1952, she was filled with a strange detached feeling, and felt she was about to foresee something important. Sure enough, she saw the White House and, above it, the date 1960. She saw a man with blue eyes and brown hair and knew that he would become President in that year. But then, she suddenly knew that he would be assassinated.

Jeane Dixon

The day draws near

Eight years later, John F. Kennedy became President. He fitted her vision perfectly. But as time went on, Jeane

kept seeing a black cloud, hovering over the White House. Then, on Friday, November 22nd, she knew the fated day had come...

The President's family at his funeral

President Kennedy and his wife minutes before the assassination

All famous people have one thing in common: other people are interested in their lives and in what will happen to them. This interest may be a major factor in explaining all the celebrity tragedies that have been predicted.

An uncertain future

Princess Diana's future was widely speculated about in the media. People wanted to know as much as possible about her. Would she marry again? Would she remain popular, or would her lifestyle start turning people against her? It's therefore not really surprising that

Photographers followed the Princess everywhere.

out of all the millions of people wondering about her future, one person had the idea that she might die in a car crash.

A likely situation

James Dean's love of speed and fast cars, along with his reckless nature, made him quite a likely candidate for a car crash. It's also possible that Alec Guiness's words were given greater significance after James's death. On seeing such a powerful car, he may have said something like, "You'll kill yourself in that!" without meaning it literally.

The problem is that his words were not recorded. We don't know, for example, what tone of voice he used to warn James. It's common for people to re-interpret memories

The young Alec Guinness

after an event. Alec's grief at losing his friend may have led him to believe he had given a more specific warning than he really had.

Prepared for office

A closer look at President Kennedy's life makes Jeanne Dixon's predictions less remarkable. His father, a former US Ambassador, had groomed him for office from an early age, so it is not surprising that she predicted he would become President.

His assassination was not so easy to foresee, but it was still not altogether unlikely given the political unrest of the 1950s and 60s in the United States.

Joseph Kennedy, John F. Kennedy's father

ESP AND IDENTICAL TWINS

Many identical twins claim to know what the other twin is thinking, even when they are apart. But does this suggest that twins are more psychic than other people?

Separate lives

Although they grew up together, identical twins Jan and Sue had lived apart for several years. Sue married and moved from England to Australia, while Jan also married but stayed in England.

A painful event

One day, Jan was at home when she felt a terrible pain in her lower abdomen. She was sure it had something to do with Sue, and told her husband so.

Later that day she phoned her sister in Australia, and Sue's husband answered. He told Jan that Sue had suffered a miscarriage earlier in the day, and had been in a lot of pain, exactly where Jan had been in pain earlier.

Unusual closeness

Identical twins are often brought up to do everything together. Other people – even their parents – are often fascinated by their similarity and actually encourage them to act as one person instead of two. This often leads to a closeness which is beyond most people's experience. As a result, both the twins and the people around them can tend to believe they are psychic.

No firm evidence

This attitude may explain Jan and Sue's story. If Jan was used to linking her experience with Sue's, she might assume that the pain in her abdomen was also linked in this way – but it may have been a coincidence.

In ESP tests, it has been shown that identical twins do tend to think in very similar ways, but that their psychic ability appears to be no higher than anyone else's.

Could twins' minds have a special connection?

ARE ANIMALS PSYCHIC?

On April 14th, 1865, so the story goes, President Abraham Lincoln's dog started running around the White House, barking furiously. It had never done this before. Then, later that day, as the President sat watching a play, he was assassinated.

Some people claim that the dog knew what was going to happen, but is that really likely?

Some birds use the position of the sun and stars to navigate.

Amazing abilities

Animals have many abilities which seem astonishing to humans. Fish and birds can find their way over thousands of miles. Dogs can be trained to respond to the slightest signal. Some dogs, for example, have been trained to help people who suffer from fits by detecting when the person is about to have a fit before they know it themselves.

Salmon can smell their home stream even in the sea.

Explanations

Explanations have been found for many of these abilities. Animals often have highly developed senses. It's known that salmon find their home stream, after spending years in the sea, by using their sense of smell. It's also possible that a dog's acute sense of smell can detect chemical changes in humans, indicating things such as excitement, fear, or a fit that is about to happen.

Mysterious skills

Some people still claim that animals can detect things which would be impossible to detect with their senses. The story of President Lincoln's dog is one example. Another which has been investigated recently is the psychic ability of some dogs to tell when their owners are on the way home. Dr. Rupert Sheldrake is a scientist who is particularly interested in this.

Jaytee the terrier

In 1994, Dr. Sheldrake was contacted by dog owner Pam Smart. Pam was sure that her terrier, Jaytee, could tell when she was coming home, and would

Dr. Rupert Sheldrake

show this by going to the front door to greet her long before she arrived. Dr. Sheldrake agreed to investigate.

Video cameras were set up in Pam's home. Jaytee was observed every time Pam started out for home, with the astonishing result that he went to greet her at the door 80% of the time.

Over the course of the tests, Pam went home at different times and in different vehicles.

Pam claimed that going to the door was Jaytee's special way of saying that she was on her way home.

Other interpretations

Other investigators also tested Jaytee. They noted that Jaytee went to the door many times during the day, not only when Pam started her journey home. They concluded that there wasn't enough evidence to prove Jaytee's psychic ability.

Human assumptions

How can we tell who is right? It's very difficult. One major problem with attributing psychic ability to animals is that humans can't question them about their motives. President Lincoln's dog may have foreseen his master's death; but it's also possible that he was spooked by something completely different.

We can never be sure exactly why a dog is barking.

Case study seven: CRISIS APPARITIONS

A "crisis apparition" is a particular kind of vision – usually of a person who is dying, or in some kind of trouble, at the moment it appears.

Date: December 7th, 1918
Place: Near Scampton Airbase, Lincolnshire, UK

A MAN AT THE DOOR

The date was December 7th, 1918. Two friends in the British Royal Flying Corps met up in the morning at their base in Scampton, Lincolnshire. One of them, Flight Lieutenant David McConnel, was to fly off on a routine mission to Tadcaster, 60 miles (95km) away. His friend, Flight Lieutenant James Larkin, was staying at Scampton.

It was a dull and foggy December day, but the pilots were used to flying in poor weather.

"I'll be back in time for tea," said McConnel.

Back early?

At 3:25pm, Larkin was in his room when McConnel opened the door. He had obviously just got back, because he was still in full flying gear.

"Hallo boy," he said to Larkin.

"Back already?" said Larkin. He was surprised that McConnel had done the trip so quickly, especially in the fog.

"Yes," said McConnel. "Got there all right. Had a good trip." The friends chatted for a few minutes. Then McConnel said,

"Well, cheerio." He shut the door and left.

McConnel stood in the doorway with his hand on the doorknob.

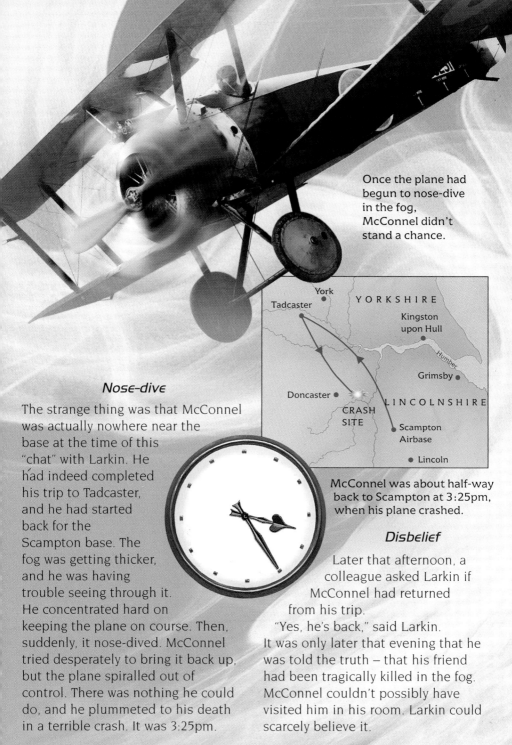

Once the plane had begun to nose-dive in the fog, McConnel didn't stand a chance.

York
Tadcaster
YORKSHIRE
Kingston upon Hull
Humber
Grimsby
Doncaster
CRASH SITE
LINCOLNSHIRE
Scampton Airbase
Lincoln

McConnel was about half-way back to Scampton at 3:25pm, when his plane crashed.

Nose-dive

The strange thing was that McConnel was actually nowhere near the base at the time of this "chat" with Larkin. He had indeed completed his trip to Tadcaster, and he had started back for the Scampton base. The fog was getting thicker, and he was having trouble seeing through it. He concentrated hard on keeping the plane on course. Then, suddenly, it nose-dived. McConnel tried desperately to bring it back up, but the plane spiralled out of control. There was nothing he could do, and he plummeted to his death in a terrible crash. It was 3:25pm.

Disbelief

Later that afternoon, a colleague asked Larkin if McConnel had returned from his trip.

"Yes, he's back," said Larkin. It was only later that evening that he was told the truth – that his friend had been tragically killed in the fog. McConnel couldn't possibly have visited him in his room. Larkin could scarcely believe it.

Case study seven: CRISIS APPARITIONS

Date: January 3rd, 1856
Place: Mississippi River, USA

MRS. COLLIER

Mrs. Collier woke up suddenly, her heart pounding. There was someone in her room. A man – standing at the foot of her bed.

"Joseph!" she exclaimed. It was her son. She sat up, horrified. His face! It was so badly cut, and disfigured, and there were bandages all around his head. Why was he there? He should have been in command of a boat on the Mississippi River, far, far away.

Then he disappeared. Mrs. Collier was totally bewildered. What could she have seen?

Mrs. Collier saw Joseph in the first light of dawn.

A fatal collision

It was January 3rd, 1856. Joseph Collier was on board his riverboat, very early in the morning. The sky was still almost dark, although the eastern horizon was growing lighter. Mist hung over the water, and visibility was poor. Joseph stood on deck, directing his crew as they peered into the gloom. The boat moved slowly down the river.

Suddenly, another boat loomed up out of the mist. Joseph desperately shouted orders to his crew, but it was too late. The boats smashed into each other.

A Mississippi riverboat like the one captained by Joseph Collier

The falling mast

The crash broke one of the ship's masts. Joseph saw it too late. The mast fell and knocked him over, crushing his skull and killing him.

Two weeks later, Mrs. Collier heard the tragic news. She remembered her vision of Joseph. It must have appeared just as the mast fell upon him.

Date: January 1970
Place: Vietnam

BONNIE MOGYOROSSY

For Bonnie Mogyorossy, what began as a pleasant evening with friends turned into the night of a chilling vision.

Bonnie's fiancé Don was away from the United States, fighting in the Vietnam War. On the day of the President's annual State of the Union address, Bonnie and her friends decided to spend the evening

President Nixon giving his address in 1970

together. When President Nixon began his speech, they settled down to watch it on TV.

A nightmare on the screen

Suddenly, Bonnie saw something strange happen on the TV. The President was disappearing, and a jungle scene was appearing instead. Then, to her horror, she saw a person lying on the ground in the middle of the scene. It was Don – shot dead. Then a voice pounded through her head, saying,
  "He's dead. Don is dead."

The terrifying vision of the Vietnam battlefield was all that Bonnie could see on the screen.

A fit of hysterics

Bonnie burst into an hysterical fit of crying. Her friends turned to her in amazement – a few minutes earlier, she had been perfectly happy.

Bonnie told them what she had seen. Her friends couldn't believe it, as none of them had seen anything of the sort. They assured her that she must have fallen asleep during the President's speech and dreamed it.

When she had calmed down, Bonnie began to think they might be right, and she tried to forget about it.

Terrible news

A week later, Bonnie received the news of Don's death. He had indeed been killed in action in Vietnam... on the very night that Bonnie had seen him on TV.

Case study seven: THE ASSESSMENT

There are three main schools of thought about crisis apparitions. The first is the sceptical view that they are imagined, or invented, by the people who see them. Another view is that the person in trouble sends the image, suggesting that the apparitions are a type of ghost. The third view is that they are caused by ESP – the receiver picks up a telepathic message, then somehow visualizes it.

Figments of the imagination?

Crisis apparitions often appear to a close friend or relative of the person in trouble. It is possible, therefore, that it is anxiety about the person which creates the mental image. But the McConnel case cannot be explained by anxiety, as Larkin had no particular reason to worry about his friend. Also, this doesn't explain why the apparitions nearly always coincide (often almost exactly) with a major trauma of some sort.

Mrs. Collier's case offers another curious angle on this theory. She saw bandages around Joseph's head. Even if she had been worrying about him, it seems unlikely that she could have imagined the precise details of how he had been injured.

A kind of ghost

The idea that the apparitions are a kind of ghost, sent by the person in trouble, does seem to fit Mrs. Collier's story. Joseph may have wanted her to know what had happened to him on the boat.

The ghost theory does not really explain Bonnie's experience, however, as Don did not appear in the room where she was; she saw a vision of the scene of his death.

Lieutenant Larkin's vision is also problematic. If Lieutenant McConnel sent an image of himself, why would he have made a mistake about his own death, saying that he had had "a good trip"?

Telepathic vision

The telepathy theory seems to work best for all three stories. Larkin may have had a strong impression about his friend without realizing that it signified his death. Bonnie Mogyorossy could have "seen" what happened to Don telepathically. It even explains Mrs. Collier's vision of Joseph. If she sensed his death telepathically, she may also have picked up how it happened.

MODERN ESP TESTING

Scientists continue to carry out different kinds of tests for ESP, and to develop new techniques for doing so.

Restricted response testing

Some scientists are still using the techniques developed by Dr. Rhine (see page 15), but they have refined them to make them more accurate. This sort of testing is called "restricted response" testing, because the subjects are tested on specific targets such as Zener cards.

Free response testing

Other scientists use "free response" tests. This involves letting the mind run free and allowing images to form. The target in these experiments is something more complex than a simple shape, such as a scene or a short video clip.

Ganzfeld technique

In free response testing, it is thought that people perform best if their minds are free of distractions. A popular way of achieving this is using the ganzfeld technique.

The subject lies down comfortably under a red light. White noise (a gentle "ssshh" sound) is played through headphones to cut out other noises. Half table tennis balls are placed over the subject's eyes, to create a soft pinky-red light.

A "sender" transmits a randomly chosen target image, and the subject is asked to describe what comes to mind. This is then compared with the target image.

A researcher assessing results

Success or failure?

The overall average for test results is just above what might be expected by chance. Therefore, many experimenters think that ESP may well exist, but if it does, it is very weak and unreliable.

Someone ready to take part in a ganzfeld experiment.

TEST YOUR OWN ESP

It's quite easy to carry out ESP tests of your own. You can try two types – a restricted response test, and a free response test.

A restricted response test

You need to make a pack of Zener cards, either by photocopying page 15 and cutting out the cards, or by making cards and drawing on the shapes. A pack contains 25 cards, so make five cards of each shape.

Setting up the test

You need a friend to be the sender. You are the receiver, or subject. You both need a pen and paper on which you write down numbers 1-25. It's important that you can't see what your friend is doing, so sit back-to-back. Your friend takes the pack of Zener cards and shuffles them, then starts turning them over one by one, making a note of the order in which they appear.

The sender uses a knock on the table to signal that she is about to turn the next card.

For each card, your friend signals when it has been turned over, and you write down which card you think it is.

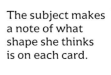

The sender should look at each card for a few seconds.

When you have finished going through all 25 cards, compare your guesses with the real order of the cards. Give yourself a score out of 25. Then, your friend shuffles the cards thoroughly and you do the test again.

You should do at least three tests like this, and work out your average result. The more tests you do, the more accurate your average result will be.

The subject makes a note of what shape she thinks is on each card.

Assessing your results

To find your average, add up all your correct answers. For example, for four imaginary tests:

$$8 + 7 + 3 + 6 = 24$$

Divide this sum by the number of tests that you did (four):

$$24 \div 4 = 8$$

This imaginary average is eight.

The odds of getting the answers right by chance are 5-1 (five out of 25). Scientists have worked out that you need an average of nine out of 25 to demonstrate ESP at work.

How accurate is this test?

This test is not as strict as it would be in a laboratory, but if you do it enough times without cheating, your average should still be fairly accurate.

In laboratory testing, the subject and sender sit in different rooms, to avoid the risk of giving away clues about the cards. The signal to move on to the next card is given electronically, for example with a light. Machines called Random Event Generators (REGs) are used to shuffle the cards, so that their order is strictly random.

A free response test

Once again, you are the subject and a friend is the sender. The sender chooses four different pictures and places them in four identical envelopes, without you seeing them.

You sit in one room while the sender sits in another and shuffles the envelopes, then opens one. The picture inside is the target.

The sender focuses on the target image for about five minutes, while you draw whatever comes into your mind.

The three unseen pictures, or "decoys"

The target image / The subject's impression

An example of a free response test

Assessing your results

The sender now opens the other three envelopes and mixes the four images up, then comes into your room and gives them to you.

Decide which of the four images looks most like what you drew. Look for correct shapes, for example square or circular things, as well as for correct objects.

When you have decided which picture your impression is most like, the sender can reveal which picture was the target.

Do the test several times, then work out your average result. The odds of guessing the target by chance are 4-1 (25%), so two right out of every four tests would be a good result.

INDEX

The publishers are grateful to the following organizations and individuals for their permission to reproduce material:

(t=top, b=bottom, r=right, l=left)

p4 (both) Topham Picturepoint; p5 (tr) Topham Picturepoint; p7 (footprints) W. Perry Conway/Corbis; p9 (tl) Topham Picturepoint; (tr) English Heritage Photo Library; (b) English Heritage Photo Library; p10 (br) Camera Press; p11 (tr) Topham Picturepoint; (b) TRH Pictures; p12 (r) Topham Picturepoint; p13 (both) Jeff Roberts, News International Syndication; p14 (l) Mary Evans Picture Library; (tr) Mary Evans Picture Library, Society for Psychical Research; p15 (tl) Topham Picturepoint; p16-17 (scene) Tony Stone Images; p16 (skiers) Lisa Miles; p17 (t) Topham Picturepoint; p19 Tony Stone Images; p20 Paul Broadhurst/Fortean Picture Library; p22-23 (mountains) Topham Picturepoint; p23 (br) Associated Press; p25 (both) Associated Press; p27 (bl) Mary Evans Picture Library, The Cutten Collection; (r) Allan Hobson/Science Photo Library; p28 (tl) Camera Press/ILN; p29 (tr)Camera Press/ILN; p28-29 (Titanic) Twentieth Century Fox, still courtesy of The Ronald Grant Archive; p30 (b) Mary Evans Picture Library; p31 (tr) Camera Press; (bl) Mary Evans Picture Library; p32 Mary Evans Picture Library; p33 (br) Camera Press; p34 (tl) Warner Bros. (courtesy of The Ronald Grant Archive); (tr) Topham Picturepoint; (b) Pictorial Press; p35 (tl) Corbis-Bettman/UPI; (tr) Fortean Picture Library; (r) AKG London/AP; (b) Corbis (UK); p36 (l) Rex Features, Julian Makey; (tr) Mary Evans Picture Library; (br) Hulton Getty; p38 (tr) Robert Harding Picture Library/Minden Collection; (bl) Tony Stone Images; p39 (tl) Dennis Stacey/Fortean Picture Library; (bl) Jane Burton; p40-41 (t) TRH Pictures; p42 (r) Sylvia Pitcher/The Weston Collection; p43 (l) Associated Press; (on screen) AKG/AP; p45 (tr) Guy Lion Playfair/Fortean Picture Library

With thanks to Stefan Barnett, Michèle Busby, Neil Francis, Mark Howlett, Asha Kalbag, Jan McCafferty, Ian McNee, Jonathan Miller, Susannah Owen, Fiona Patchett, Joe Pedley and Mike Wheatley